# Joe's! Job! Journey!

**This is fictional but it's the truth!**

**This is A lie but I ain't lying!**

Written by: Joseph Earl Brathwaite SR.

Illustrated By: David Eric Hampton

# Chapter: ONE

Now as you begin to read about my journey. I must make one thing perfectly clear. I am the hardest working man in America! But unfortunately I'm also the Worst employee from America! I am no killer going all postal and shit! I'm no pervert or under the desk  wack master or a walking sexual harassment!

I am a misunderstood black man! I'm Walking the line of a harsh work environment. Now with that said and out the way you should feel my feelings when I say.

---

---

A job, A job! What the hell is that? I'll tell you what that is. It is a piece of fucking shit that you have to put up with day in day out or die! Or go hungry, or homeless! All that is out the way for the time being. Feelings are important!

Now a job is far more different than a career. A career is something that brings good money not just barely enough money like a job does.

A career can bring happiness and fulfillment a feeling of being needed and appreciated. Now a job. Ha Ha Ha! funny stuff huh. A job can also fill you up with something, but not with LOVE but horrible zombie shit!

That is what you have to deal with on a job.

First of all let me teach ya something. A job does not really need you or else, they would not be willing to get rid of you so easily. A good wolf always got sheep at the gate! The only need a job has for you is to use you!

Secondly, why would they appreciate somebody that they are using? They appreciate the cheap labor that's all!

Thirdly, a job only will provide enough money for your hard worked services to pay your bills, but not enough to really live. Got to keep them peasants way down on their level in the dirt!

Now let us begin our journey folks. The sun beats down on the backs of a Mummy and her youngest baby. He is a 13 years old a golden brown,  handsome!

Chocolate black teen boy

named **JOE**!

They are working in the front garden planting rose bushes and various other flowers. Now Joe has always been a landscaper in training. His wonderfully smart Mother has taught him many things he will need in life to be a real MAN!

Now just like there are differences between a job and a career. There are also many differences between a real Man and what “Kevin Hart" calls a “Mitch” or male Bitch!

Now this kid Joe’s MOM was raising him to live real as a Black Man in America.

He was well trained in etiquette, landscaping and other career oriented things.

But was he ready for this world as it is?

Or was he only ready for the world

that the schools taught him?

Joe's very realistic MOM thought he should be prepared for all the traps that life surely had setup for him. She knew that the Schools were only teaching ABC's and 123's and a bunch of Half lies all in between.

They made slavery ok, like black people like to work for free!

Bullshit! Waghington did not lie Bullshit again! Was he or was he not a politician? He was not the first President but he did get in like all the rest of them. From the first all the way up to "obama", "Trumpy '' and "Crazy Joe Biden"! It is not the people that are picking the country's leader. It Is a small group of citizens, called the Electoral College.

So with such lies running the world Joe's MOM had a plan one day. She Told Joe that the family car was junky, a real pig sty as she often said referring to Joe's room.

She also stated that she lost a $100 dollar bill somewhere under all the car's mess. He could have $100, if he cleaned the car inside and out. Starting with washing the car. Joe jumped at his MOM's offer!

He thought to himself finally a paying gig instead of all this free slave lawn care stuff. Joe hard cleaned that car. It was only a busted Cordova, but it was clean as a Bently.

Joe was very happy with the great work he did to his MOM's car. But strangely enough he did not find that dang $100 but all the same he was excited with his first solo assignment completed.

Joe started to jump around and sing I got a job, I got a job I am the Man, I'm the Man. He jumped and sang his way into the house to find his Mummy! Hey, Hey, Hey Boy what you doin? Joe stopped jumping and replied your car is all clean, your car all clean.

But no hundred dollars! No hundred dollars! But Joe still needs to get paid, Joe needs to get paid!

His MOM broke out laughing and said there ain't no missing $100 dollar bill in the car I tricked you like most jobs will!

I got you to not only clean and vacuum the inside, but also you washed the car. That is not funny, MOM Joe says.

Yes it is says MOM you was with me earlier this morning when we went to the car wash. HA HA HA! you was so amped up to get that money you forgot. HA HA HA! I sold you a false promise and you paid above the price.

HA HA HA! MY golden brown boy do not get mad. I have taught you an important lesson.

In life the world will always sell you a false hope, especially a job. They will tell you how much they are different from other companies.

They will lie to your face and say we are family, we got your back if you have problems. They will sell you a wolf ticket if you let them. Joe stood there for a second then said oH I see MUMMY.

Life is going to try and play with me on this work stuff Huh? Yeah they will, Son. We "gotta play the game if you wanna win". That is the lottery slogan MOM.

WEll it should be for life too. I Will just say this: if you want a job you will get it, but if you want a career you gonna have to work your jelly. Meaning you're gonna have to work harder!

You black in a place that does not want you to succeed. So spread that jam boy you understand me. Yes, Ma'am Joe says. I fully get it MOM! Joe did get his Mommy's point. But will he remember when face to face with the world?

The next paying position Joe got was through his Nana. Who by the way was a big gangster in her own right. She got Joe hooked up! He was gonna work the summer school break as an attendant at the local city pool.
And yes it was a hookup job, Joe was only 14 years old without
any working permits. Nana had the juice!

So Joe started his new job at the city pool. Now this particular pool was no ordinary poor kids pool. Oh no it had all the hood stars from the flyest dresser to the most paid drug pusher and all his minions. If you was the dopest dancer you were at the pool with your boom box on deck.

And OOOOOOH all the pretty girls! And trust me when you're 14 years old and all the girls are in bikinis, none of them are ugly they are all very, very pretty.

Joe loved his first real job! He thought to himself watching all the Beauty and Booty pass by while working the check in desk. This is the career for him.

The most gorgeous of all the girls, where the lifeguards, they were all female. Joe's older sister was the head lifeguard. She was very loving and protective to her little brother. She saved his life!

When Joe was 5 years old, he and his sister were walking in the dirt poor projects where their Mummy had an apartment. All of a sudden a german Shepard attacked little Joe chomping down on his upper leg!

The dog picked him up and was thrashing his leg like a wild gator! Joe's wonderful and pretty sister, Remember She was head Lifeguard, a person born to save. She beat the brakes off that dog till he released her kid brother. So she was one of his heroes and he trusted her word!

Plus she kept him fly by combing his nappy head every morning before school. She made sure his clothes were tight and on point at all times! Joe’s Mom’s had three jobs and left before the kids did everyday.

Now back to the pretty people's job that JOE had at the pool. One of the Lifeguards was movie star pretty and Joe had a crush on her!

She was so pretty he looked at her even when She did not wear a bikini. Whenever she caught him looking she would smile and wink. Joe never took it seriously though she was a senior in highschool and he was in the eighth grade.

He got kept back or should I say his Mom"s made them keep him back. Joe was kind of a Class Assclown but he got over it on his journey towards manhood!

One day another Lifeguard caught Joe looking at his pretty Lifesaver. She surprised him, and said you know She like, likes you. Joe said no way she said yes sir, way!

She wants you to meet her in the locker room, you down little guy? Yeah Joe whispers and runs to the locker room! When he enters the room he screeches to halt right in front of his chocolate Lifesaver.

She says Hey I see you got the message. Joe says uh uh looking deep at her gorgeous eyes. She really likes me, she really likes me, he thinks in his head. He starts to tell her how pretty she was and how he liked her hair and what not.

JOE was talking and Before he knew what was happening  she gave him one long deep Ass kiss. Joe's toes curled up it seemed and a shiver went down his spine!
She backed up smiling all flirty and ran away.

Joe was just stuck there for like 5 minutes! Later that day she asked Joe if he wanted to come to a party? Acting all grown he said Hell yeah!

When he got home he took a shower and started to get ready for the party. While he was getting ready for the party his sister passed by his room. She said, where you think you are going? He said that the pretty Lifeguard from the job kissed him and invited him to a party. She said What and got really angry!

## She a set up bitch JOE!

He said what HUH? SET up what? She said you wait right here mister party kissing man. She stormed out the house talking to herself and cursing! I'm gonna kill her this Bitch!

A couple hours passed by and Joe's sister returned. She said the party is canceled and you just quit that wack Assed job! Joe said whaat, why, why NOOOO!

Booty and Beauty career why?

His sister said quite boy! I beat that bitch up bad she was setting you up for failure! She the one in the hood gang in the area that lured young guys to join them!

She would half way sex up teen boys. Then She would literally Mind FUCK these youngins. And the tripped out thing was that she was only a youngin herself at 17 years old. I told our boss you quit! Right? AS she gave him the look. Ok, ok , ok sis you ain't gotta beat me  up too.

Joe Really had respect for his big sis.

She saved his life again!

That was also his first example of somebody playing games with him at a job. See, told you a job ain’t shit! First real one away from Mummy and what did Joe get? A Big pile of Zombie shit.

# Chapter: TWO

Now the next position that Joe held was much different than a job or a career. Let's start it this way. It was a dark rainy Monday morning a black boy walks through the rain with an umbrella that looks like it ain't stopping much rain.

He is headed to his New school.

I take that back he is headed to the Bad kids school, which is his New school since he got kicked out of the old one! I told you Joe is kind of a Class Ass clown but he does not do it on purpose. But he was good at it, a Class act at being Bad in school.

He earned the Class to his Ass Clown by doing Bafounary that his peers had never seen before! Sometimes he just does not think, he just acts! Now let's flash back to the old school JOE just got expelled from!

**{Scene Change}**

We are at The Franklin Redfordman Middle school. One class room is on fire, but not with flames. In walks the Principal of the school. He is very angry, he surveys the classroom and sees that the whole class is out of their seats!

They are hooting and howling, laughing and jumping around all out of control. The Spanish teacher was in the corner hysterically crying her eyes out!

In the middle of the kids acting all wild is Joe! He is being restrained by the big burly black English teacher!

What in the Hell is going on here MR. Falsy? The principal Belches out! The English teacher answers all out of breath still trying to restrain Joe. This kid is very disrepectfull he has been a Smartass to the Spanish teacher Ms. Frenchy all year!

And now he spit a paper spitball right down her throat during her lesson! While she was gagging it up he encouraged the whole class to riot!

He passed out straws and all 24 kids commenced to Assault Ms. Frenchy with nasty spitballs. It was like a plan he came up with to get revenge on her for all his detentions.

Yeah I know about all the trouble Mr. Joseph has been giving Ms. Frenchy this year, the principal said!

Mr. Falsy said that is when she came to me crying for help. I entered the class and had to restrain Joe. He was on the teacher's desk dancing while the other kids cheered!

You's a DAMN liar Mr. Falsy! It was Art paper spitballs Joe said while pulling a hand loose and slapped the teacher with a full hand! The room said ooooooh! Mr. Falsy's eyes turned Blood red and JOE swore he saw an explosion of fire deep in his pupil!

Joe was too bold. He said what you gonna do now Bitch! Heads flew back including the principal and the whole room went OOOOOH Daaamn! Real loud.

Mr. Falsey must have lost his teacher's mind. He grabbed the hand that slapped him and slammed Joe down face first onto the teacher's desk by his hand, and proceeded to try and break Joe's arm! With another loud OOOOOH Shit it's gonna break from the crowd! The principal screamed NOOO!

You Crazy Man, he's a child! And pulled Mr. Falsy off of Joe before he broke his arm. You could hear a slight cracking sound, but the child did not scream. He just had the OOOh shit! It's gonna break face! 2 seconds before the principal pulled MR. Falsy off of Joe.

He screamed your fired falsy, and your Expelled too MR. JOE! Two violent acts with one blow!

## Chapter Three:

That is the story Joe told  at the bad school when the teacher left the room. The other kids asked why you here? Joe was an honest kid so he told them the truth. After telling them his school boy crimes Joe asked what brings y'all here.

One kid said I don't like school so I took the math teacher's car to go get weed and got into a police chase and crashed it up.

Another boy said I put Bleach into a water pistol and spayed five older kids in their eyes! They were bullying me real Bad and I had enough of that shit!

The funny thing though, was that they were in five different classes.

So I went class to class and found their eyes. Security did not catch up to me until I was on the last guy. I got him real good he was their leader and I broke the water pistol on his smart Assed mouth! The rest of them laughed.

Joe said what brought the rest of y'all here? Weed they all said in unison. Joe laughed his ass off!

Now let's get to this work that was not like a job or a career. Joe sat in his new school which was really weird. On each of the kids' desks there was an astray and you could tell they were in use by the amount of ashes still present and the smell.

The teacher was giving an English lecture while writing on the board and smoking a cigarette. His desk also had an ashtray on it. What a school Joe thought. This is Where do the bad kids go? Huh this place gonna make me even badder!

Now this school also had an unusual lunch procedure. The teacher would pass out the school issued lunches to the kids then he would leave for an hour. The kids could either stay in school or go home or world for an hour. That was a lot of responsibility for a Bad Assed Middle schooler! But it is what it was back then.

Joe was only in the New bad school for 3 maybe 4 weeks. Close to Summer when a new kid came to the school.

Let's just say he was much different than all the other Bad boys. His parents had a lot of money and so did he. He did not respect his Parents especially his Mommy or his Prep school so he took a Shit on the Headmasters encyclopedia collection. For fun and to piss OFF he said!

It made all the boys laugh when he told us why he was there, but for Mr. Bleach water pistol and Mr. Car chase guy. All they saw was a disrespectful to his parents wanna be, Bad kid. A privileged Asshole who needed to be taught a lesson. They was really respectful to they parents, especially their Moms. It's just the school and the world that they lacked respect for.

So they set a plan into motion to rob him in school! So they waited until lunch when the teacher and most of the other students and other staff went to lunch. They convinced new kid to stay by promising him a Weed lunch in the little library the school had.

Now Joe was a little naive to real Crime. So when  the plan went into motion MR. Bleach, whispered in Joe's ear, we gonna rob this guy!

This ain't no FUCKING Weed lunch JOE, you keep watching! So now you get it right? The work that aint a job or career but still pays good.

Joe thinks about it. He didn't like **n**ew kid either, he talked meanly about his Mummy, I mean his own birth Mummy!

Joe got real serious when he heard that whisper, but this was about to be the funniest SHIT he ever seen!

Mr. Car chase walked over and smacked **n**ew kid's ham and cheese sandwich out his mouth as he was biting it!
Sending it crashing into the wall!
He said Hey guy why you do that?
That was my FUCKING lunch!

Mr. Bleach said you know why Bitch run them pockets! **n**ew guy said Hells No to Mr. Bleach! That's when Mr. Car chase punched the hell out of him, so hard that it made his chin hit the table and flung his chocolate milk in the air!

Now Mr. Car chase's punch hit him so Hard it made him fall to the ground as well. They both slammed on the floor with chocolate milk showering both of them!

Mr. Bleach picked up one of the library books and started beating new kid in the head, like he was trying to force a book full of words into his brains! The hardway.

Joe was watching the door doing his work well as always and watching this “3 Stooges” ASS whooping!

Mr. Car Chase was on the floor wrestling with the **n**ew kid who was trying to fight back. Mr. Bleach was trying to hit **n**ew kid with the book in the Dome, but for some reason every time he swung for his head, the book only hit him in the butt! And every hit kept making his pants fall.

So imagine that scene, three teenage guys fighting covered in chocolate milk, one hitting the other in the BUTT creating a plumber BUTT situation. It was a Classic comedy moment.

Joe said Alright, Alright let's get on with it when the plumber BUTT appeared while he laughed!

They took this kid's money! Something like $112 dollars only because he bought some extra lunch stuff chips and candy bars and SHIT for $3 dollars. They took that too, snacks and All! Joe got his share. It was fair.

But we must beware being a Robber comes with a certain Snare. It's Addictive! You make Madd,Madd money, and want more can't stop won't stop your eating like a Big Pig. Until the real PIIIGS end up catching your robbing ASS!

Robber Man says, this is the worst SHIT. A BULLSHIT Gig that gets me locked! But it's not a job or career. It's putin in work, gettin a lick, It's catching a NIGGAH whenever one slips! It's something to have Fear of So, PLEASE don't live like this!

new kid never told he had a little bity gangster stuff in him. He finished the school day out Watching the whole class eating his snacks. Even the Smoking teacher ate a few chips! **n**ew guy sat with a funny look on his face, and Big Fat ASSED lips.

He Never should have talked about his Mummy like that and SHIT! He brought it on himself! He never came back to that school though. And who knows what happened to Mr. Bleach and Mr. Car chase? BIG ups to my dudes! FEAR THE chase & Just LOVE TO RACE! YOU MUST Remember always. JOBS ain't SHIT FAM!

# Chapter:FOUR

Now Joe's next Job wasn't really a job that paid money. It paid by showing Joe a new world! Joe was always well liked at the school that he got kicked out of and he still had friends. One of his best friends was a musical King in the Hood.

He made really good Rap beats.

The King Invited Joe to a Rapp show at a local hood bar. Joe was surprised by the location of the show; he was too young to go into a bar and so was the King! The king assured Joe that the show was legit for them to be there.

Being Deceitful, Joe learned this on his own that day! He made the plan to do his homework, clean the dishes, take care of the dog, take out the trash and do any chore his Mummy could possibly need to be done. When all the chores were done.

Joe Made his Mummy a hot cup of chamomile tea. Joe knew that she always fell fast asleep after her tea. Of course She went to sleep, She had three jobs. Damn! Let me say it again, a job ain't shiiiit!

When his Mummy was fast asleep Joe Snuck out the house to the 5 corners Neighborhood where the bar was at. It was a real quick walk. The bar/ Dive club was only a couple of blocks away.

When Joe entered the bar he was in shock! More than half of his Old class was in the bar, with drinks in their hands and smoke blowing out their mouths. Joe shouted this Place is the SHIT!

He made his way around the bar giving Pounds and Dapps to his old classmates. He finally made it to the main bar and he sat down at a stool. The bartender came over to Joe and said what will it be guy? Joe paused and said, UUUH I don't know, I never ordered a drink before.

THE bartender said all the other kids ordered Hennesey on the rocks. Joe Said yeah that is what I want. In his mind Joe was like you gonna give me Rocks to drink? LOL! And what the HELL is Hennesey?

He said we shall see I'm grown as SHIT in here. He looked around and saw the other kids were smoking big "Cubano" Cigars and drinking with the adults that were in the bar. He said HUH we all grown as SHIT in here Tonight! When the bartender gave Joe the drink he looked at it and paid for it.

Then he started laughing at himself **{on the rocks}.** Joe finished off the drink and started to make his way to the little stage in the back of the room. Joe stopped next to one of his homies who was Blowing Back a fat ASSED Blunt. His homie was like, you Smoking tonight?

Joe was like HELL yeah pass that! Joe was feeling Himself, he got a real drink for the first time and now the first blunt in public!

He was flying in space by the time he noticed that the King was DJing and a young rapper was going off on the microphone. Joe said yeah this is what's up he was dancing all wild with a girl to the harcore rapp beat.

He was in LOVE with the career that the king and the M.C. were pursuing. Now this is what's Good they don't got a job and it is better than a career, it's life! Joe really was enjoying his Grown ASS night.

He went back to the bar about 4 times for more of them Rocks and liquor! Joe SHUT the bar down all his friends were gone. He stumbled out the door swerving like he was a drunk driver!

It was the longest walk back even though he got there very fast. His feet did not seem like they wanted to move fast. Joe finally made it home; he dragged his heavy feet up the stairs trying to be quite stumbling the whole way up.

He finally made it to his room and passed out face first on the bed. He had really good Dreams thinking about his Dream gig or Life as he called it. Because as we all know a job aint shit to Joe!

## Chapter Five:

Now the next job Joe had was Cold as Ice! He worked in an Ice Cream Parlor chain, that shall not be named to protect the Innocent business from its Bad Employees Shame. Joe and his coworkers ran that place into the ground.

They all were really Bad employees, but they had a lot of fun and they were really good for the customers.

They treated this chain restaurants guests better than they ever did!

This restaurant ice cream parlor was not that busy a place maybe 12 tables and a small ice cream bar. Joe was one of the 3 teenaged waiters.

They had two beautiful lady managers in their early 20s! One did the cooking and the other handled the paperwork in the back office.

They both were very freaky ladies, free spirits who appreciated the staff and customers. At The end of every day when they closed the restaurant they turned the store's audio system onto some really Amped up music. These sexy ladies danced around smoking Weed with these teen workers!

After about a month they Fired one of the teens for being a BITCH! That is what they actually said to him when he got Fired.

They told Joe and the other employee he was going to tell on them for Partying every night after they closed.

Now WE can not have that! Right? Right, right the teens said!

Plus it's time we told yall we been Robbing the restaurant, the Manager that works the office said! Us too Joe and his coworker both Shouted we been pocketing every other table and Voiding the checks in the cash register.

WE now the Manager that cooks laughed! Yeah and I have been Cleaning your Mess up for a while, the office manager said!

We were just waiting for the right time to tell y'all. We got rid of that BITCH so we are good now! Now this went on for a long while and the Managers started getting more freaky with their workers.

They all had good times together, they CUTT {really liked} for their teen Crime workers and really cared for their Party Boys.

The cooking Manager would pull out both of her TITTIES, all pretty, fluffy all in the Dish pit letting Joe feel her up. The office Manager was always grabbing Joe's BUTT. Feeling his Manhood strong and hard in her hand! One day the office Manager asked Joe to pull his DICK out. She said she never seen a brown one! Joe said OH MY! Show me a TITTY or BUTT first. This Manager was shyer than the other one, so she moved slowly. She smiled and stood up from her chair and turned around and Exposed her whole Naked BOOTY!

She pulled her clothes up and sat back down. Right before Joe could get his hands on her Lovely goods. She said your turn looking at Joe’s Junk waiting for a Peek.

Joe said ok you ready for this?

She said yeah come on Strip,Strip,Strip Man.

Joe was a little bit shy about doing this because when she showed her Back parts it Turned him on a lot so he was Big.

She said come on, come on!

Ok here it comes! Joe pulled out and slapped it on her desk right on the paperwork. She said Damn Impressive for a young guy!

Just as she said that the door Flew open! The cooking Manager and the other employee came in. They was like what do we have here? Looking at Joe with his big member on the desk and the office Manager smiling she says nothing as She is giggling!

Doing some paperwork! As she continues laughing. Joe hurried and put it away pulling the stuck papers of his Member! He did not want his man coworker to keep looking at his better side. He zipped up and laughed.

That was some fun. They all laughed and turned the music up to dance around. That was one of the best jobs that Joe ever had!

But It seems that all good do things come to an end though! Eventually the company had to close its doors. The Staff were stealing too much and the restaurant was not making any money anymore so they closed the branch. All the workers and the freaky Managers went their separate ways and they never got caught for stealing and Partying hard with teens . They treated that Job like a JOB usually treats their employees. They bled that BITCH Dry and moved on when it was all used up! Just how most Jobs do their employees. HA, HA, Ha JOB justice for Joe!

Now this Job truly was the SHIT, but the company didn't give a Big Zombie SHIT about loyalty and employee commitment.

So once again A Job ain't SHIT, this was the bestest,  but one like this no longer Exists!

# Chapter: Six

Now the funny thing about Joe's next job is that it was working in the same restaurant Ice cream Parlor that he just stopped working at. It was maybe like two weeks after that, he got the new JOB. So when Joe started working there he knew exactly how to work the system.

The only problem was that Joe's new boss was a real mean DICKHEAD! Instead of 2 Beautiful Freaky Managers!

He would give Joe a lot of SHIT about any little thing. Joe you're Five minutes late, Joe your Uniform is Wrinkled, Joe your Shoes ain't Shiny Enough. Damn he was harsh!

Joe hated his JOB and so did his homie from school Rich THE DOLLAR MAN that’s what he liked to be called. They both were working the system. Every other table got put in the Pocket and a Void check was written in the register!

These boys were on their game Both of these teenaged highschool workers worked real hard. They were the waiters, cooks, cashiers, greeters, Ice cream scoopers, sundae makers and Janitors. And MR. mean ASSED manager just sat his fat old Self in the office all day giving every worker SHIT! He was not a Racist or anything like that, he just was not a Happy man!

Joe often looked at his boss and thought. Man, your Life and Wife at home must be SHIT! Is that why you so Damned mean In this Ice Cream BITCH! Joe always had Bars and rhymes on his mind since he was at that bar in 5 corners! Remember that is Joe's dream JOB or LIFE as he calls it.

One day while working Joe's friend RICH THE DOLLAR comes to work all excited! Halloween night and RICH THE DOLLAR was telling Joe It's a good night to get a LICK Man catch a NIGGER while he slips!

He had been talking to Joe for weeks about robbing people in the neighborhood where the two teens worked in.

It was a very rich and upscale neighborhood, Joe was a little skeptical he had never robbed nobody before just been a  lookout on a couple of scores. But after a while it started to make perfect sense to the crime part of Joe's mind.

Well I’m making money working here, scamming the register more money here. Hell yeah RICH THE DOLLAR said lets rob them hit Licks and get BUCKS here!
So the two teens worked their full shifts at the JOB, got their paychecks and each one had  pockets full of register scam cash.

They went to the nearest supermarket to cash their checks and get Halloween Masks. It was ON! They left the store quickly and went down an alley that led over to the next street.

AS they walked through the alley Joe and his homie put on devils Masks! How fitting for the night and for what these teens are about to do!

They pulled out pocket knives as they came out the alley a lady saw them and she ran off scared and screaming! Joe whispered to RICH THE DOLLAR Hey man no Women. OK?

For sure RICH THE DOLLAR SAID I Loooves women not robs them! They both chuckled then went back to work.

Now Don't get it wrong this was not a JOB in the Hood. This was called puttin in work! The teens were far from home doing this risky SHIT!

So the next guy RICH THE DOLLAR SAW he ran up on him and had the knife at his face saying run them pockets. All before Joe could react and then it was over. RICH THE DOLLAR was a 17 year old professional stick up kid Joe was a rookie!

You got that dough quick, Wardy. That’s what I do! RICH THE DOLLAR said, now let's keep it going. It's still pretty early in our Halloween crime night!

Next one is all your’s Joe. OK let's go get it. They were very excited, Wilding out a menace to the rich peoples neighborhood! The young men robbed ten victims that night RICH THE KIDS all time record.

Joe did his solo to prove he had heart then they partnered up. One knife on each side of your face picks up the money pace. So in no time the teens had RICH THE DOLLAR's magic number 10. RICH THE DOLLAR had a look on his face he said 11!

11, Yes, Yes, please one more to break the record. Ok Joe said the last one man my feet hurt. Stick up kids do a lot of running Joe out of shape! Joe and his crime buddy stalked around for the Coudigrah victim!

They saw one guy coming out of an ATM they moved in to get him. As they was nearing the target he noticed the two devil faced teens approaching!

He screamed I ain't got no money, my card Declined! NO, NO, NOOOOO It surprised the teens, all the other vics were quiet and just shook a little bit, But this guy he was a mess. He was crying and moving back and forth a lot! Then he did this weird zig zag thing and took off running!

The teens gave chase but were no match. He was like they say “crackhead fast”. Yeahhhh and you “ain't catching no crackhead” that’s a Hood rule! They smokin the devil's fuel. The teens stopped running to catch their breaths and laugh. Joe said DAMN he was like a fast crack addict athlete RICH THE DOLLAR giggled out loud.

Just then the teens could hear Police sirens heading their way. Oh SHIT one time, 5/0, them 12’s Joe said let's go!

Run NIGGER I ain't gettin hit! They ran down the block and took a right. They both ran dead into a real big guy. He was really surprised! They pulled out the knives and RICH THE DOLLAR said run those pockets big boy!

The vic said in a high pitched girly voice NOOO don't hurt me take the money! The teens looked at each like whaaat the FUCK, your voice!

He gave it up to RICH THE DOLLAR money from every pocket repeating please don't hurt me. The teens silently giggled then took off running again! 11,11 RICH THE DOLLAR was Hooting, OH my SHITS 11!

Joe suddenly noticed a little girl there were in front of in a window frozen in place staring at his devil mask as the teens ran away. They left her stuck in the window and left big boy crying in his hands, stuck himself, to that robbery spot on the street!

You could hear the sirens getting closer so the teens pushed it into Hyperdrive! Joe was running faster than he ever did before and he could feel he had much more to give for Freedom's sake.

The teens ran really hard turning right then left trying to take the fastest way to MAINFRAME ST. That was where the train station was.Joe and RICH THE DOLLAR had to get out of the neighborhood. They was the wrong color to be there with cops looking for robber jackers!

The teens pulled off the devil Masks and put them in their school bookbags with their homework. They took another right and had finally made it to MAINFRAME ST. They Just had to get to the station which was straight all the way.

They saw the cops take a right onto MAINFRAME ST. a couple of blocks back from where they turned onto the street! Skiiirt JOE grow wheels we got Pigs! Rich the Dollar said.

OOOOOH SHIT JOE said! Just then a limousine was coming down the street. The window rolled down. The boys were shocked at what they saw.

In this limo were a lot of beautiful debutant teenage girls all dressed up like at prom. They were  screaming and flirting with JOE and RICH THE DOLLAR.

HEY there brown sexy boys WOOOOOOO come to us. Joe and RICH THE DOLLAR started flirting back while running.

HEY there pretty ladies you so fine can you be mine. YES, YES, Yes all the girls said. Joe said stop open the doors. NO stopping, NO stopping the driver said, he was a Hating ASS BITCH. HELL with that the girl at the door said and she flung the car door open and said jump! Joe and RICH THE DOLLAR LooK back and saw “Porky The Pig” GETTING CLOSER and they said FUCK JAIL and jumped into the limo one after the other. Each teen landing face first into a pretty girl's lap!

The limo took off with the cop car going around traffic with sirens blaring and the spotlight searching!

Freedom! Joe said out loud. What you say the girl that he landed on said? OH Joe said. You ladies are like freedom to these poor field hand NIGGAH'S! Both teen boys and the girls laughed wildly. As they drove down MAINFRAME ST. It was a Hot Sexy party in a limo, music blasting and all.

The girls were still flirting and kissing on the boys. They invited the boys to a Socialite party that they were going to in NEW RICH PEOPLE Ville. NAW, NAW NOW Joe said my lady! Kissing the girl he fell on, but now she was in his lap now saying AAAH come on, it will be fun.

Joe knew the world's reality though he could get caught up by other cops in that neighborhood too!

Having that chocolate handsome brown skin could bring Bad SHIT.

So Joe said another time, another party shorty.

Plus look at our clothes. We just got off work we on Grime Ball status instead of our usual Fresh to Death! She said yeah you are right. Joe said, driver stop here at the train station let us out.

The teen boys hugged the girls, got their phone numbers and said see y'all Lovely ladies soon. Bye guys we'll miss you the girls said blowing kisses and waving.

The teen boys ran to get a train that was pulling into the station. They sat in a rear car and started pulling money and wallets from their pockets. It all fell onto the train seats and onto the floor. Everybody on the train looked in their direction.

There were a lot of coins from their tips at the Ice cream restaurant, but mostly Dead president bills. Big Faces!

YEAH Joe shouted! RICH THE DOLLAR laughed and said I told you Joe. We're gonna have a HELLA day off from work tomorrow! That’s for sure Joe replied. The train rolled down the track shaking the boys and their pockets full of money.

The teens made about $500 a piece from their Epic Halloween robbery spree! Another $150 a piece from jacking tables at work,$65 to $ 75 dollars in tips a piece, plus a full week of money on their checks plus credit card tips coming on next week's check.

Joe thought about the number of people they got it! All that fear left on the streets and the number of dollars in his pocket.

The whole night in general he remembered thinking all the way home! But he could not get that Terrified look that the little girl had on her face off his brains.

He realized that the little girl had seen the whole Robbery Go Down! She was watching Joe and RICH THE DOLLAR in devils Masks robbing the big boy! It worried Joe that they had mentally Traumatized the poor little thing.

He had no remorse for the 11 men they Robbed, they are MEN they will get over it and it’s life's traumas that build Men or “Girly men”! Joe had a gangster mentality, but he was a gentleman at all times he called it his “Double GG standard”. No woman or child will get hurt on my watch. Joe thought in his mind “Double GG “All the time!

So that little girl in a window watching robbery plagued Joe for years. He knew not who she was to make amends or wipe away tears.

He fell into the trap, a Monster Robbery Addict he didn't listen to his own caution words he had no fear of the Evil trade!

The next morning Joe woke up feeling good but Strange. Before he could try and think about that Feeling the phone rang.

Hello Joe said in a sleepy voice, hardly holding the phone. Who dis?

It's RICH THE DOLLAR what goody boy?

Nothing much Joe said just woke up man.

What's good with you? It's all good here man he said all excited and full of energy!

I have been up thinking and planning our next LICK or VIC if you like vic better. I told my big cousin what We were doing last night. He's an old school stick up kid.

He said what the Hell cuz you can't be hunting with a knife. So he let me hold a 22 and a 25 caliber pistols so we can live good on the job! OH YEAH Joe said.

Listen, my Dude robbery is not on my career goals path I'm gonna have to pass.

It was Madd fun though a real thrill ride. I kind of figured that Joe. RICH THE DOLLAR said it's ok, but taking away is my way the career for me.

I'm past the crime Addict level you warned me about. But everybody gotta be who they be! "YEAH BOOY" he said like "FLAVA FLAV" on stage!

When Joe went back to work RICH THE DOLLAR did not come in. Joe called his Homie on his break, but the line was disconnected. Joe tried calling many times but the line was always disconnected. RICH THE DOLLAR even disappeared from school!

Nobody knew what happened to him, but Joe always thought that his dream JOB did him in or the cops locked him in!

Either way RICH THE DOLLAR, Joe's Crime partner came to an end and Joe never saw his Homie again. It also seemed like Joe's ice cream parlor restaurant job was coming to an end also.

Joe's boss seemed to be getting meaner and meaner since RICH THE DOLLAR disappeared!

He could not find a replacement for him. The pay was shit! That is why the teens started to rob the place. A whole bunch of Slave work for Slave pay.

So now that lazy ASSED FUCKER had to come out of the office to help. He was really mad about that and started to take it out on Joe and the rest of the employees.

His favorite word was faster, faster. He was also known for telling the Females to stop dragging their Big Ole ASSES.

And right in front of customers! He would tell his workers, you aint SHIT I should Fire your BITCH ASSES!

He had no respect for the workers. This was a real SHIT JOB! Run by a real live wire SHIT HEAD! For some reason he never cursed at Joe. He must have smelled his street Thug stuff. He was just on that faster, faster SHIT!

One day Joe was coming out of the kitchen with a full tray of food for a table 5 plates heavy. When he opened one of the swinging doors his foot hit a pile of butter tabs that some ASSHOLE worker dropped and didnt clean up!

Joe slid from that door across the restaurant through the seating area and passed the stunned customers all the way towards the window!

He barely was able to stop inches from crashing through the window, but Joe's momentum kept the plates of food moving on the tray. So Joe stopped sliding and the plates of food flew off the tray, crashed through

the window and doused a car that was outside of the window with food and glass!

Joe said OH SHIT with the tray still balancing in his hand. What dumb fuck dropped the butter? It got quiet and Joe scanned the room. His eyes bugged out and he said

YOU, YOU. Staring and pointing at his BOSS holding a bowl of butter tabs and a big spoon. I,I,I the Boss stuttered!

I, I my ASS Joe said then he verbally laid into the guy with no remorse.

This tongue lashing was building up in Joe and now he was gonna get it.

Joe said you FUCKING sorry example of a manager, I don't want you to suck a bag of DICKS, because you are a bag of DICKS! And by the way you do smell like a bag of Funky nastiness take a shower sometimes you Funky Fucker!

You BITCH Ass boss. Why you gotta be like this Wife not FUCKING you any more? By now the whole staff is laughing at the The boss really hard and pointing!

Joe had a college vocabulary and knew how to fight with his words especially with swears. The BOSS really got madd his eyes and skin had a bright red tint to them.

He looked like a volcano erupting and He jumped up in Joe's face screaming your Fired! Joe says Fired HA HA HA!

I just Quit Bitch! By definition Fired sounds like a Violent Act, like a Bullet being Fired from a gun trying to kill you. Take your life! The word Fired hurts and kills makes you live a homeless man’s drills!

So this BITCH boss committed a Violent act towards Joe by attempting to Fire him even though he was already Quitting until being rudely interrupted.

Joe fought back with an army of foul words arguing in his now ex-boss's face. The argument got so heated that the Boss tried to punch Joe. Now how low can you be? To be an adult trying to hit a teen, a kid,a child!

Joe ducked the punch and watched his ex boss fall into a dirty table face first busting his ASS as he fell through the table and plates!

Now that's a Violent act, Joe laughed while walking out of the restaurant. Joe turned and looked at everybody and said, yall see that Violent act this NIGGER just Fired himself!

HAAA, HAAA, HA! The whole restaurant employees and even the customers with food on their forks burst out laughing and pointing at Joe’s ex Boss!

One guy said you knocked yourself the FUCK out trying to hit a child. Yous a BITCH and a Coward laughing hard in the ex-Boss's face! He just laid there in shame as Joe danced out the door!

## {SCENE Change}

The next Job that Joe got he had this Job twice once in the day and once in the night. It was a Job that was good to Joe but Joe was not good for the Job! He worked in retail clothes sales. Joe did not mess with their money or their customers,

just their clothes.

At first he worked for them on the overnight shift. A very weird shift they had only during Christmas time.

This store was a skyscraper, but Joe worked in the basement and that was fine. AT least he didn't lean He worked at night with a bunch of other teens from 10pm to 8:30 am.

He had to be at High School by 9.  Joe was a damn hard worker even during that time. Joe knew what he was worth to the company.

He was nothing but cheap labor. Joe folded the clothes that got messed up during the sales day. He also put clothes back on hangers for the next day of business. It was a really busy shift while the store was closed.

Joe had one main boss that he met with on Fridays. This guy was all business, no fun at work type. Joe was happy that he did not work the night shift with him. He was too strict and no fun. Joe thought that must be how he lives his life, all boring and SHIT.

Joe only had to see him to get his check and get his work schedule for the week. The Assistant Manager was really cool. He was from Joe's hood.

He let the teens come to work late, drunk, high and even let them bring their girlfriends on Saturdays. AS long as the JOB gets done at the end of the day I don't care what you guys do. He would always tell us this as he would leave every night with a joint in his mouth.

A month had passed by on the overnight shift when Joe noticed that they could do whatever they wanted at night. The Assistant Manager really was not kidding. The teens ruled the store at night; it was theirs outright!

When Joe noticed how lawless it really was OH boy what a feeling! Fred the Man was coming down the escalator with an arm full of fur coats.

Joe said why you upstairs? I thought we could not go up there. NAW Fred the Man said we run this Bitch our way at night. That's the hustlers way the Assistant Manager knows.

That's why he leaves every night, so we can have at it. He doesn't get the blame the customers do and he gets his cut. Cut Joe said what cut? Fred the Man said Damn boy you nieve! The cut of the money when we sell the stuff on the bootleg market in the streets.

OH, OH Joe said I get it. He smiled really big and said I'm gonna be a bootlegger! Yeah you are FRED the MAn said, just watch the cameras. Your boring ass boss watches it in the daytime. The guy doesn't have a life or a wife, so I guess it's a SHIT life for him.

Joe laughs and shrugs OH well. Time to get my legging on  Joe chuckles! He starts with short sleeved POLO shirts, hats, ties and any small expensive items that will sell fast in the streets. His little side hustle was paying off big.

The kids at Joe's school were the ones buying most of his bootleg stuff.

The streets bought a little of his ill gotten loot, but mostly his classmates. Joe went to an international high school so the kids were from everywhere. Somewhere black some white some Indian or native American, Asian, Spanish, Amish, German, Dutch.

Joe had friends of every kind he knew how to keep in touch. He was a peoples person and was well liked. Except by those who wanted a fight or to hate on Joe because he shining too bright!

It was a good gig the last week of work before the new year. The teens threw a big blow out party right inside the store. There was an exclusive guest list  and Joe's old friend The KING DJed.

All of downtown had the loud sounds of bass speakers bumping hard Rap music. It was so DAMNED awesome!

The cops tried to shut them down but could not because the teens were very smart. They were letting the people in through a service door that was in the train station. So 5/0 only saw people going to take the train, which was normal.

The Christmas JOB was over after that, but they kept 3 teens to work during the day.Joe was one of the 3, but this time he was putting on tags so nobody could steal clothes. How Ironic is it that a teen bootlegger was stopping people from stealing!

Joe's life was Hectic school work , gang work, house work, homework, work work, hustle supreme “money on his mind and his mind on his money”.

He done seen his Mummy working too hard 2 and 3 JOBS all the time. Not my life, not for mine he thought this often but he would find out he was wrong. Life doesn't give a SHIT gotta be rich to make it through this life's bullshit! SHIIIIIT And I don't mean money rich like dollars or pesos.

I mean rich in strength of mind to make it through this poor black man mess. Stress kills fast like a Diabetic that can't control his Anger!

There is a big danger a JOB will break your heart and change a worker for the worse.

Now the new but old JOB had its good and bad parts. The good thing was all the Bootlegging stealing SHIT. The Bad part was a SHITTY boss once again for JOE! This guy would always tell JOE's crew to work harder, work faster.

If you can't keep up then get out! He even told his workers, I'm a hungry wolf and you little sheepies better move faster or you will get eaten up!

The worst part is that he was always trying to make them work harder for the same money. He never worked hard. He would be sitting at his desk the whole time Barking his little inpatient orders from his cubicle in the corner.

Lazy MOTHER FUCKER JOE often said under his breath. The Boss did not hear him but JOE’s co workers always heard him talking SHIT to his supervisor. It tickled the HELL out of them and they would bust out laughing all the time!

The shitty Boss would be like Hey, Hey shut that SHIT down. You ain't here to laugh and joke .What the FUCK you think this is? Then he would yell that this is a MOTHERFUCKING JOB!

Not a MOTHERFUCKING playground! Get the FUCK back to work before I Fire the FUCK out of all you sorry workers. This guy was a really harsh guy with no remorse or mercy!

So Joe came up with a plan. This BITCH boss had to go; he had no respects in him. It had been the industry standard for the guys in the theft prevention department to open boxes and put tags on all the expensive Clothes and pocketbooks.

The whole team was liberating different items from the store, but they would only take a small amount so It was not noticed.

The new plan involved taking too much so they would look at DICK the boss in a Bad way. The loss prevention team took all the POLO, Gucci, Luchi foo foo rich people stuff. They put the high end merchandise in a garbage container one item at a time throughout their work shift. By the end of the shift they had thousands in the garbage ready to move.

This was not about greed, it was payback! Joe and his work buddies  even sold the stuff for the cheap and even gave some away. The garbage bags were huge, filled with Ill gotten loot and a little bit of paper. The boss was not Efficient nor did he pay much attention to detail.

He was just a loud rude ASSHOLE that some fool put in charge. He did not even do his own paperwork.

After each box of clothes was tagged and hung up he was supposed to check that all the merchandise was there. Then he would sign and date the inventory sheet stating all goods were present and tagged and on a hanger on the rack.

The lazy loser always had Joe's coworker check on the merchandise he would just sign without checking the Job himself. When Joe learned that he did This. He knew how to get that BITCH! The whole staff wanted him gone. They just had to stick to the big plan.

A couple of weeks passed by and the corporate office people noticed that a lot of goods were not making it to the floor!

It was coming in on the truck, but never making it out of the Loss Prevention room. They never had any proof on the workers. All roads were leading to the boss.

After all, he signed the inventory sheets saying that all goods were tagged and hung for sale.

He didn't handle his duty right so they Fired his behind quickly. The day he cleaned out of his desk and told the team he was let go, he tried to be mean to them , but Joe stopped that. He said hurry up and get yourself gone man. Hurry up and get the FUCK out you've been Fired!

IT's like he got shot by an embarrassment GUN. No pain, NO blood, but it hurts your heart a Violent Act all the same. Joe sang “Shame on a boss NIGGER when he try to run Game on a teen and his team now get the fuck out”!

The whole loss prevention team was laughing and pointing at him! He grabbed his stuff to leave and then he looked at Joe with a Death stare. You gonna get yours youngin he said it again. You're gonna get yours! Yeah right JOE said just leave Loser!

# Chapter: Seven

The team celebrated with a little bit of liquor and a little Bluntage. They were all happy the wicked BITCH was gone.

Joe went home late that day.

He was at work till late at night time celebrating getting rid of that guy.

Joe was a little tipsy when he got off the City bus. He was walking the 5 blocks to his house. He was almost home.

When suddenly a Black car screeched in front of JOE and blocked his path pulling onto the sidewalk.  Guess who it was?

Yup your right it was the BITCH boss man. He jumped out the car with a bat in his hand and grabbed Joe and threw him on the car face first. He said you're gonna pay for what you did to me kid.

He held the bat up and said I’m gonna beat your face till I'm satisfied boy. And the way I feel you might be Dead long

before I’m satisfied! Joe Looked around at his surroundings and noticed he was by the Ruford P. Rufson Elementary school. Joe went there when he was really young, like 6 or 7 years old when he was a Good boy.

Joe started laughing out loud and Disrespectfully towards his old boss! Who had no Idea he was in the Lion's Den smelling like fresh meat! and blood! What's funny you little MOTHER FUCKER? Ex-boss says!

You foolish NIGGER you on my set Joe said, my turf, my gangs playground and you the Opps! Dumb NIGGER Joe said he laughed again laughed, then he did his gangs call really loud OOOH, UUOOOH! OOOH!

His ex Boss paused then said HA little boy What the hell was that shit? You'll see come on "Big Billy The Badass bossman" start beating me BITCH Joe screamed in his face!

Oh yeah I will kid he raised that bat and came down hard on JOE's back 3 times real fast! Joe shuttered in pain but he didn't Scream like little BITCH!

**{Said in old spanish Lady voice}**

The ex Boss says OH where your boys no hel_? Before he could say that P a mob of teenagers were coming from all directions straight at him and Joe. He released the boy, and screamed in a funny girly voice.

Somebody Help MEEEEE! And he ran through the only space available as the teens were rapidly approaching and circling around him! He ran hard like an "NFL" rookie trying to prove himself to Coach.

He did not get back in his car; he ran right past it.

He couldn't get in too many teens!

"DO GOOD THE WHEELMAN" jumped in the EX boss's black car. He was the gang's driver. He always had a Hot box. The teens did catch up to him when Big MUNCHY cut him off at the corner!

I suppose this Ex-boss must have some Big Nuts his Wife don't want. Because this SHIT got him out here fighting with gang members about to die!

He reached on the ground and grabbed a long metal thing that had fallen off of some Hooptie car. Big Munchy was backing him down screaming I'm gonna crush your SHIT up NIGGER!

EX boss yelled back up, back up swinging the metal thing around back up! He quickly turned around and threw the metal and ran behind the flying object! The teens moved out of the way of the spinning piece of steel. It was big.

As the gang ran to get out of the way of the huge piece of metal coming. One of them slipped and fell and now that deadly, spinning chunk of metal was gonna hit him hard in the head! He was the youngest of the little gangsters at 8 and a half.

They called him “THREE CLAPS”! Instead of jumping him in because he was so young. They had him put work in! He did three drive bys with the big homies in under an hour with a little .380 pistol!

He had no time to get up so he tried to shield himself with his arms, but as the metal was coming at him it still looked like the kid was gonna get murdered!

Suddenly “Freddy SLAP A NIGGAH”,

he was the rapper in the crew.

JOE told ya he knows some NIGGAHS right?

But anyways “FREDDY SLAP A NIGGAH”! Stopped moving out the way of the metal and ran dead into it! He was older he could take it. It smashed him with a loud BHAANG in the stomach and dropped him just right in front of “THREE CLAPS "! He was spitting up alot of blood and coughing loudly!

The EX boss ran right past the fallen boys. He did not make it out of the circle of Milishush teens! They were grabbing him and clawing him, Punching him in the head!

They were literally kicking his BUTT and legs with booming "Tae Kwondo" kicks and punches! Joe was beating the SHIT out of him with an "Old ENglish " 40oz bottle.

He was hitting him everywhere on his body with the bottle. He told his Mob gang to watch out!

He moved in close and started clubbing the EX boss in the head with the hard bottle! 1,2 Smash 3,4 smash on the 5th one the bottle smashed over his head! Blood and what little beer that was left poured down this man!

JOE stepped back for a second to get some air. A kid came in with a Log just smashing him in the face! The gang swarmed on him, dealing out punishment from every direction! He could not fight back. This was a pure rage fulled wilding out session!

People die when gangs get down like this. The EX Boss brought this on himself. He should have stayed home Fired! And now he’s not even getting jumped!

These children were trying to kill him! They were beating him down the block all the way to the liquor store and this dude would not Die!

"DO GOOD THE WHEELMAN "

screeched around the corner yelling get the FUCK out the way i'm gonna run this Motherfucker over!

The teens scattered out the way of the speeding car, leaving EX bOSS swaying from all the teen fists and JOE'S bottle to the head.

He was a deer in the headlights as the car was coming for him!

“DO GOOD THE WHEELMAN"suddenly swerved to avoid hitting the liquor store. But he was able to smash the guy with the back of the car hurtling him through the glass window of the liquor store.

Some of the bottles from the window display instantly shattered as his body flew through the glass!

Others that didn't break were rolling around on the ground and the teens started to get as much of the drink as they could. As the gang ran around looting the liquor store!

This guy slowly was getting up! One by one the gang notices him starting to stand again. OH Hells Naw"THREE CLAPS" yells as he gets out the passenger seat of the EX bOSSES car. He grabs one of the rolling bottles from the pavement, opens it, takes a long swig, and says DAMN that's nasty!

He smashes the bottle on the ground and pulls out a little 6 shot .25mm pistol!

He cocks the gun and runs toward EX bossman firing all the way up to him!

This was a killing ASS 8 year old gangster! The last 2 shots he pressed the hammer right into his stomach. Joe saw his coat blow back as the bullets came out! That's a dead ex boss there! "Freddy Slap A NIGGAH" said! A Dead clown is the only good clown still spitting up blood as he talked everybody ran into the night!

5/0 was sure to come after them shots rang out. This went on for 35 minutes, because it was really late at night. Time to lay low for now.

Early in the morning Joe got up and watched the local news. He was a little worried about last night. They could link it all to JOE, after all he was JOE'S EX boss. Joe was sure they murdered him! But there was nothing on the news about it. Not newsworthy enough Joe thought.

I guess Just NIGGERS killin NIGGERS, Now back to the weather Chuck! Joe had to see the aftermath for himself. It was late and Dark he had to see. As he neared the corner to turn towards the liquor store.

He imagined that there would be police, ambulance fire and a lot of Dead boss blood! To JOE'S surprise there was none of that! The only thing he saw was the old owner of the liquor store sweeping glass by himself. Joe walked over asking what happened?

The owner said some drunk ASSHOLE broke into my store, knocked out my surveillance system, cut himself up pretty Bad and stole about 25 bottles of Vodka.

Damn Joe said people ain't SHIT!

Yeah the old man said.

As JOE left he noticed 6 bullet holes in the store wall, lined up going down the wall, but there was no blood from shots Fired. The last two holes were right next to each other, damned near the same hole!

Joe walked away with a troubled look on his face. No Police, No Ambulance, No News people, No body and not enough blood! What the FUCK? GOD definitely did not let him die by their hands!

That was the fifth time God had saved young JOE'S eternal Soul and fragile body. With many more mercy's to come from his Loving Lord who has a mighty patience as JOE'S JOB JOURNEY!

CONTINUES!!!!!!!!!!!!!!!!!!!!!!!!!!!!!!!!!!

---

www.ingramcontent.com/pod-product-compliance
Lightning Source LLC
LaVergne TN
LVHW091048150826
845673LV00002B/501

* 9 7 9 8 2 1 8 1 3 9 9 0 2 *